A Visit from St. Nicholas
And Santa Mouse, Too!

Clement C. Mouse
Illustrated by Loretta Krupinski

Hyperion Books for Children
New York

'Twas the night before Christmas,

when all through the house

Not a creature was stirring,

except for a mouse;

The stockings were hung by the
chimney with care,
In hopes that St. Nicholas soon
would be there;

The children were nestled all snug
   in their beds,
While visions of sugarplums
   danced in their heads;

And Mamma in her kerchief,

and I in my cap,

Had just settled our brains

for a long winter's nap,

When out on the lawn there arose
   such a clatter,
I sprang from my bed to see what
   was the matter.
Away to the window I flew like
   a flash,
Tore open the shutters and threw
   up the sash.
The moon on the breast of the
   new-fallen snow
Gave a luster of midday to
   objects below;
When what to my wondering eyes
   should appear . . .

But a miniature sleigh and eight
  tiny reindeer.
With a little old driver, so lively
  and quick
I knew in a moment it must be
  St. Nick.
More rapid than eagles his coursers
  they came,
And he whistled and shouted
  and called them by name:
"Now Dasher! now, Dancer! now,
  Prancer and Vixen! On, Comet!
  On, Cupid! On, Donner and Blitzen!
To the top of the porch, to the top
  of the wall! Now dash away, dash
  away, dash away, all!"

As dry leaves that before the wild
hurricane fly,
When they meet with an obstacle,
mount to the sky,
So up to the housetop the coursers
they flew,
With a sleigh full of toys,
and St. Nicholas, too.

And then in a twinkling I heard
　on the roof
The prancing and pawing of each
　little hoof.

As I drew in my head, and was
turning around,
Down the chimney St. Nicholas
came with a bound.

He was dressed all in fur from his
head to his foot,
And his clothes were all tarnished
with ashes and soot;
A bundle of toys he had flung on
his back,
And he looked like a peddler just
opening his pack.

His eyes, how they twinkled!
His dimples, how merry!
His cheeks were like roses, his
nose like a cherry;
His droll little mouth was drawn
up like a bow,
And his whiskers and chin were
as white as the snow.

The stump of a pipe he held tight
  in his teeth,
And the smoke, it encircled his
  head like a wreath.
He had a broad face and a little
  round belly
That shook when he laughed like
  a bowl full of jelly.

He was chubby and plump, a
  right jolly old elf,
And I laughed when I saw him, in
  spite of myself.
A wink of his eye and a twist of
  his head
Soon gave me to know I had
  nothing to dread.

He spoke not a word, but went
straight to his work,
And filled all the stockings; then
turned with a jerk,
And laying his finger aside of
his nose,
And giving a nod, up the chimney
he rose.

He sprang to his sleigh, to his
team gave a whistle,
And away they all flew like the
down of a thistle;
But I heard him exclaim, ere he
drove out of sight,

*"Happy Christmas
to all, and to all
A Good Night!"*

First published in 1998 by Hyperion Books for Children.
Illustrations © 1998 by Loretta Krupinski.
All rights reserved. No part of this book may be reproduced or transmitted in any form
or by any means, electronic or
mechanical, including photocopying, recording, or by any
information storage and retrieval system, without written
permission from the publisher. For information address Hyperion Books for
Children, 114 Fifth Avenue, New York, New York 10011-5690.

Printed in Hong Kong.
FIRST EDITION
1 3 5 7 9 10 8 6 4 2
The artwork for each picture was prepared using
Gouache, watercolor, and colored pencil.
The text for this book is set in 13-point Trump Medieval.

Library of Congress Cataloging-in-Publication Data

Moore, Clement Clarke, 1779—1863.
A visit from St. Nicholas and Santa Mouse, too! / Clement C. Mouse;
illustrated by Loretta Krupinski.
p. cm.
Summary: Presents the well-known Christmas poem, with mice characters.
ISBN 0-7868-0312-6 (trade)   ISBN 0-7868-2252-x (lib.)
1. Santa Claus—Juvenile poetry. 2. Christmas—Juvenile poetry.
3. Children's poetry, American. [1. Santa Claus—Poetry. 2. Christmas—poetry. 3.
Narrative poetry. 4. American poetry.]
I. Krupinski, Loretta, ill. II. Title.
PS2429.M5N5 1998b
811'.2—dc21   97-40335